DISNEY

ALICE
in
WONDERLAND

Mad Hatter's Tea Party

Retold by Jane Werner

Illustrated by the Walt Disney Studio

Adapted by Richmond I. Kelsey and Don Griffith
from the motion picture *Alice in Wonderland*

Based on the story by Lewis Carroll

 A GOLDEN BOOK • NEW YORK

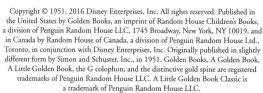

randomhousekids.com
ISBN 978-0-7364-3627-4 (trade) — ISBN 978-0-7364-3628-1 (ebook)
Printed in the United States of America
10 9 8 7 6 5 4 3

There was once a Mad Hatter, a peculiar fellow who lived in a strange little house in the woods—in the woods of Wonderland.

Nearby lived a friend of his, the March Hare. One day the March Hare heard (through the wild grapevine, of course) that it was the Mad Hatter's birthday.

So he baked and frosted a birthday cake. Then down the woodland path he went, singing as he skipped along:

"The very merriest birthday to you!
The very merriest birthday to you!"

The Mad Hatter was delighted. He called in
his friend the Dormouse, a sleepy little soul,
and what a jolly time they all did have!

They decided a birthday party was the best
of all possible fun.

The next day, the Mad Hatter kept thinking of that party and of the jolly songs they sang. He did wish they could have another party.

The March Hare was thinking about it, too. How he longed for another piece of birthday cake!

And the sleepy Dormouse wished for another cup of tea.

But it was nobody's birthday that day.

The Mad Hatter had just had his. The March Hare's was months and months away. And the Dormouse had been so sleepy when his mother told him about his birthday that he couldn't remember it at all.

"Oh, me!" sighed the March Hare. "Nothing but un-birthdays as far as I can see. It really isn't fair. Only one birthday a year and 364 un-birthdays!"

"364 un-birthdays!" cried the Mad Hatter. "Well, fine! Splendid! Let's celebrate those!"

So they did. Every day they had
an un-birthday party.

Every day they set up the table and hung up the decorations and had birthday cake and tea.

And after the party, they cleared everything away. But that soon got tiresome.

So they set up a great long table underneath the trees. They put chairs all around, and cups and plates and pots and pots of tea.

After that, they never cleared anything away. Whenever things got messy, as things at a party will, the Mad Hatter would call out, "Move down! Move down!" And the March Hare would call out, "Clean cups! Clean cups!" And away they would move, to new places at the table.

So the un-birthday party went on and on.
And every day they happily sang:

"A very merry un-birthday to you!
A very merry un-birthday to you!"

All that moving got to be too much for the
sleepy Dormouse. Since he was so fond of tea,
he just chose himself a teapot, climbed in and
stayed. Now and then he would open a drowsy
eye and join in a bit of fun.

One day, a little girl named Alice wandered into Wonderland. She soon heard singing and hurried along through the trees to see what was going on.

In through the Mad Hatter's gate she stepped. Alice saw the colored lanterns hanging from the trees, and the cakes upon the table. And she heard the jolly song:

"*A very merry un-birthday to you! To who?*
A very merry un-birthday to me!"
Then the Mad Hatter saw her. "No room!"
he cried. "What are you doing here?"

"Why, there seems to be lots of room," Alice said.
"I heard singing, and it sounded so delightful—"

"It did?" cried the Mad Hatter. "What a charming
child. Come in, my dear. Sit down, sit down."

"Whose birthday is it?" Alice asked as she sat in an
empty chair.

"No one's. It's an un-birthday party," they said,
and explained.

"Why, then it's *my* un-birthday, too," Alice said.

"A very merry un-birthday to you!" sang the Mad
Hatter and the March Hare.

"Won't you have some tea?" they asked.

"Yes, thank you," Alice said. "Just a half cup, please."

The Mad Hatter snatched up a carving knife and he cut a cup in two.

"My," said Alice, "I wish Dinah were here to see this."

"And who is Dinah?" the March Hare asked.

"Dinah is my cat," Alice said.

"Cat! Cat! Cat!" cried a horrified voice. And
the Dormouse, at the sound of that dread word,
popped out of his teapot, up into the air.

Then, before Alice even sipped her tea, the March Hare pushed her and cried out, "Move down! Move down! Clean cups! Clean cups!"

"This is the silliest party I've ever seen," said Alice. She walked out the gate and off through the woods. No one seemed to notice that she had left.

There they are to this very day, singing and drinking cups of un-birthday tea. If you should wander through Wonderland, perhaps you will find a little house in the woods and hear voices singing loud and free—

"A very merry un-birthday to you! To who?
A very merry un-birthday to me!"